GU00891721

MATCH!
Incredible
Stats
& Facts!

Another MATCH! title from Macmillan Children's Books

MATCH! Joke Book!

MATCH!
Incredible
Stats
& Facts!

MACMILLAN CHILDREN'S BOOKS

First published 2016 by Macmillan Children's Books
an imprint of Pan Macmillan
20 New Wharf Road, London N1 9RR
Associated companies throughout the world
www.panmacmillan.com

ISBN 978-1-5098-2500-4

7 9 8 6

A CIP catalogue record for this book is available from
the British Library.

Designed by Tony Fleetwood
Printed and bound by CPI Group (UK) Ltd, Croydon CR0 4YY

AMAZING PLAYER FACTS

Ross Barkley
says he'd be a chef if he wasn't a footballer!

Alex Song
has 27 siblings – 17 sisters and 10 brothers.

Maynor Figueroa

has three toes on his left foot.

Manuel Neuer

stars in the German version of the 2013 Disney/Pixar film *Monsters University*. He's the voice for the character Frank McCay!

Jose Luis Chilavert

is the deadliest goalkeeper in the game. The Paraguay international once scored a hat-trick of penalties in a match for his side, Velez Sarsfield, in the Argentinian professional league!

Rio Mavuba

was born in international waters. His birth certificate does not have a nation listed – it just says 'Born at sea'.

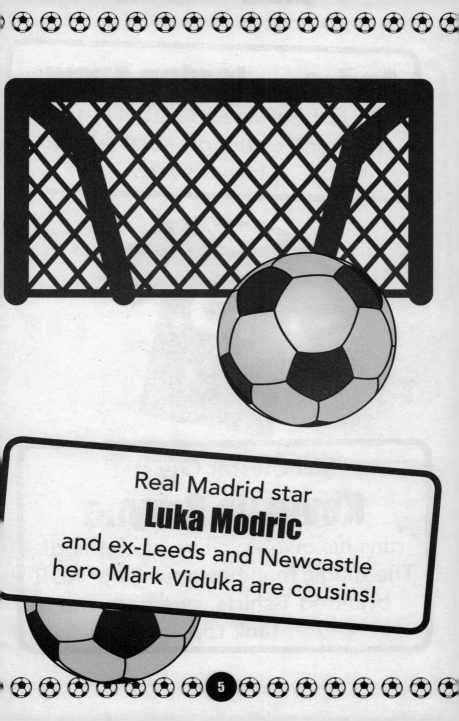

Real Madrid star
Luka Modric
and ex-Leeds and Newcastle
hero Mark Viduka are cousins!

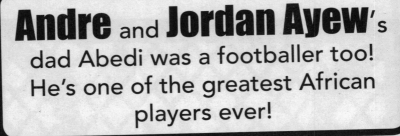

Andre and **Jordan Ayew**'s dad Abedi was a footballer too! He's one of the greatest African players ever!

Manchester City star

Kevin De Bruyne

runs his own epic line of clothing! The magic man has a range of KDB branded T-shirts, sweaters and tank tops!

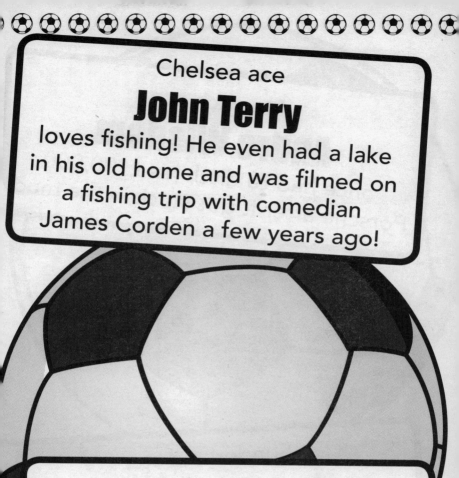

Chelsea ace

John Terry

loves fishing! He even had a lake in his old home and was filmed on a fishing trip with comedian James Corden a few years ago!

Liverpool's attacking midfielder

Roberto Firmino

used to be a defensive midfielder at youth level.

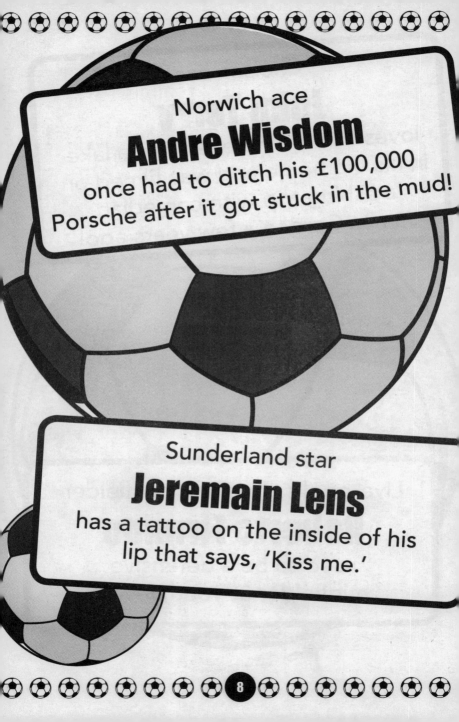

Norwich ace

Andre Wisdom

once had to ditch his £100,000 Porsche after it got stuck in the mud!

Sunderland star

Jeremain Lens

has a tattoo on the inside of his lip that says, 'Kiss me.'

Newcastle and Holland star

Georginio Wijnaldum

dreamed of becoming a gymnast when he was younger – not a footballer!

Liverpool full-back

Nathaniel Clyne

has a tattoo on his arm – of himself! The piece of ink is a picture of the defender when he was a kid!

West Brom striker
Rickie Lambert
used to work part-time in a beetroot factory when he was at Macclesfield!

Mesut Ozil
had a crazy nickname at Real Madrid – Ronaldo and co. called him 'Nemo' after the clownfish from the Disney film!

LIVE

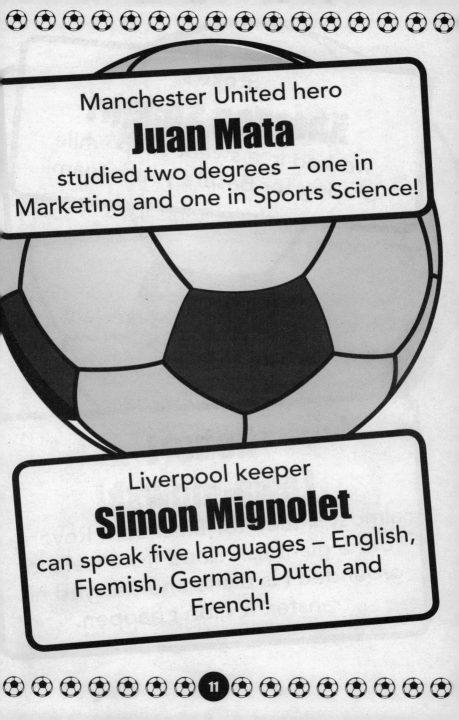

Manchester United hero
Juan Mata
studied two degrees – one in Marketing and one in Sports Science!

Liverpool keeper
Simon Mignolet
can speak five languages – English, Flemish, German, Dutch and French!

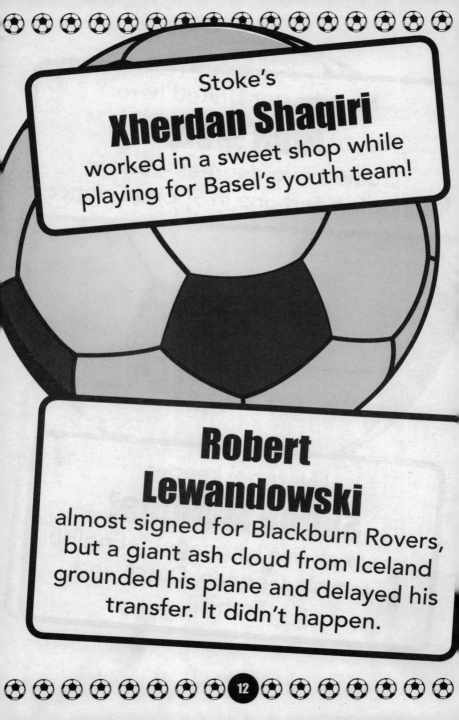

Stoke's
Xherdan Shaqiri
worked in a sweet shop while playing for Basel's youth team!

Robert Lewandowski
almost signed for Blackburn Rovers, but a giant ash cloud from Iceland grounded his plane and delayed his transfer. It didn't happen.

Liverpool keeper
Simon Mignolet
started his career as a forward,
and only had a go in goal after
he was dropped!

On the other hand,
Fernando Torres
started his career as a goalkeeper, and
later switched to become a striker.
(No wonder he became so good at
keeping the ball out of the goal!)

Diego Maradona
once played for Tottenham Hotspur!

Dimitar Berbatov's
childhood hero was Alan Shearer, and he used to sleep in a Newcastle shirt when he was young!

Lethal Everton striker

Romelu Lukaku

has always loved busting net! As a youth player, he scored 121 goals in 68 games for Lierse and 131 in 93 games for Anderlecht. Boom!

00:00 MINS

HOME   AWAY

1   0

When

Angel Di Maria

was a youngster, his mum took him to see a doctor because he wouldn't stop running! The doc told him to start playing football – not a bad decision, was it?

In 2008–09,

Charlie Austin

scored 46 goals in 46 games for Poole Town while also working as a bricklayer!

Ever wondered how Manchester City powerhouse

Wilfried Bony

got so tough? Well, wonder no more – his mum was a black belt in Judo!

Newcastle players don't need to worry about getting injured, because Magpies striker

Papiss Cisse

can help – he was an ambulance co-driver when he was 15!

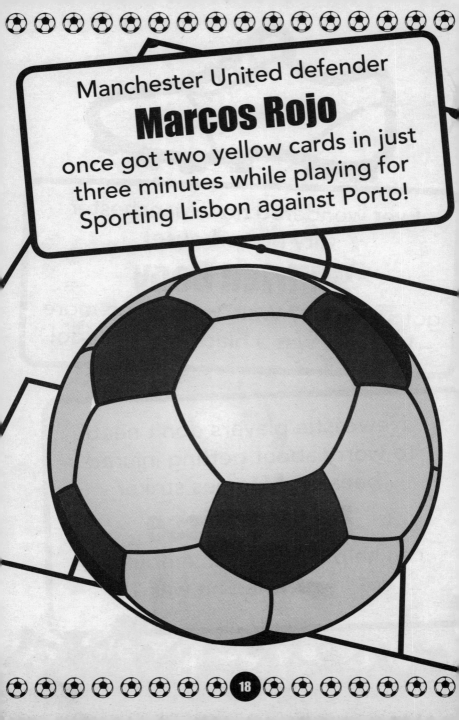

Manchester United defender

Marcos Rojo

once got two yellow cards in just three minutes while playing for Sporting Lisbon against Porto!

During his career, Brazilian legend, **Pele**, scored 92 hat-tricks, four goals on 31 occasions, five goals six times and once bagged eight goals in a game!

TICKET

Steven Gerrard has scored in the FA Cup, League Cup, UEFA Cup and Champions League finals!

Brazilian striker **Ronaldo** got his crazy haircut at the 2002 World Cup so that his son would be able to tell him apart from the other bald Brazilian players on TV!

Zinedine Zidane almost joined Blackburn Rovers, but the club chose Tim Sherwood instead, with chairman Jack Walker saying: 'Who needs Zinedine Zidane? We've got Tim Sherwood.'

Cristiano Ronaldo was named after former US President Ronald Reagan!

Peter Shilton has made the most appearances in English league football. The keeper racked up an amazing 1,005 league appearances.

Garrincha

was born with an illness that should have made it impossible for him to walk. Instead, he became incredibly flexible and agile, which helped him while playing football.

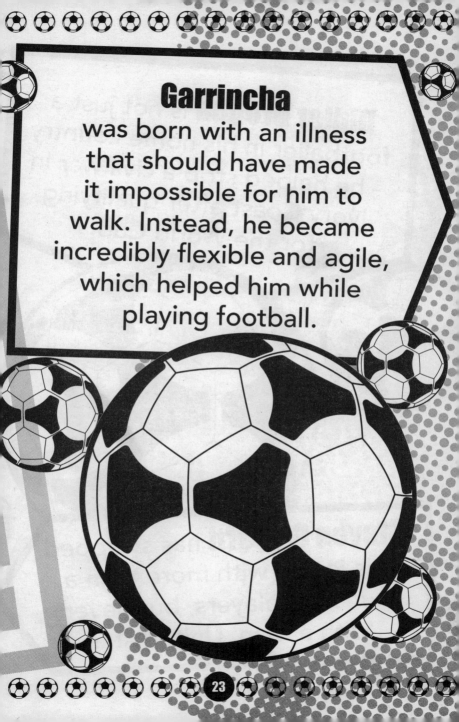

Didier Drogba is not just a footballer in his home country – he helped stop a civil war in Ivory Coast after qualifying for the World Cup.

Steven Gerrard has swapped his jersey with more than a hundred players, but never with a Man. United star.

Ronaldinho first hit the headlines when his youth team won 23–0 – and he scored all the goals!

When Man. United legend **Paul Scholes** came out of retirement briefly in 2012, he didn't have any boots as he'd given them all away so he popped to JJB Sports and bought a £40 pair to play in!

Dennis Bergkamp would miss away matches because he had a fear of flying, which is why he was called the Non-Flying Dutchman.

Arguably Finland's greatest ever player, **Jari Litmanen** holds an incredibly unique distinction: he is the only footballer to have played international football in four different decades.

THE WORLD CUP

13

Only 13 countries entered the first ever World Cup, in Uruguay way back in 1930, and many countries travelled for weeks by boat to get there!

Four months before the 1966 World Cup finals in England, the Jules Rimet trophy was stolen from a stamp exhibition in Westminster. David Corbett and his dog Pickles later found it lying under a hedge!

Brazil was allowed to keep the Jules Rimet trophy after winning it for a third time in 1970!

5

Russian forward Oleg Salenko holds the record for the most goals in a single World Cup final match. He netted five times against Cameroon in 1986!

After Brazil was allowed to keep it, the trophy was stolen in Rio de Janeiro and was believed to have been melted down! Now, no country is allowed to keep the real trophy and winners are given a gold-plated replica instead!

36

The current World Cup trophy is 36cm high, one centimetre taller than the Jules Rimet trophy.

A European team has reached every World Cup final except for the 1930 and 1950 finals.

Oliver Kahn is the only goalkeeper to win the Player Of The Tournament in a World Cup – all the other winners have been strikers!

Franz Beckenbauer is the only person in the history of the World Cup to win the title as a player and coach for Germany. Beckenbauer led the German national team to their title in 1974 as a player and won it again in 1990 as the coach for the German team!

8

When Germany reached the World Cup final in 2014, it was for the eighth time – a new World Cup record!

5

Brazil hold the record for the most World Cup wins! The Samba kings have won it five times, compared to Germany's four titles!

India pulled out of the 1950 World Cup because FIFA refused to let them play barefoot!

14

In 2014, Germany's Miroslav Klose scored his 14th World Cup goal, and overtook Brazilian goal machine Ronaldo to become the top goalscorer in World Cup final history!

3

England and Italy share the record for the most World Cup penalty shoot-out defeats – they've lost three each!

They're not exactly World Cup giants, but Australia hold the record for the biggest World Cup win! They crushed American Samoa 31–0 in a World Cup qualifier, which beat the previous record they had set just three days earlier when they thrashed Tonga 22–0!

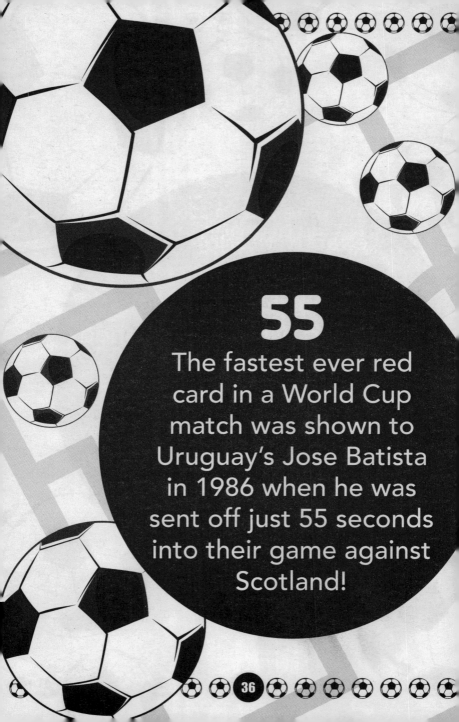

55

The fastest ever red card in a World Cup match was shown to Uruguay's Jose Batista in 1986 when he was sent off just 55 seconds into their game against Scotland!

Uruguay was the first country to win the World Cup in the year they hosted the tournament, in 1930.

20

Brazil is the only country to have played in all 20 World Cup finals from 1930 to 2014!

Imagine this –
you're in the World Cup semi-final, just about to take a penalty when your shorts fall down. A crazy dream? No – this actually happened to Italy's Guiseppe Meazza in the 1934 semi-final against Brazil! It didn't do him any harm, though – he pulled them up and stuck his penalty away to take his team into the World Cup final!

11

Turkey's Hakan Sukur holds the record for the quickest goal at a World Cup final when he scored after 11 seconds into the game against South Korea in 2002!

In 1986, FIFA stopped players from swapping their shirts after games because they didn't want players to 'expose their upper bodies' on the field.

3

Holland have finished World Cup runners-up three times, in 1974, 1978 and 2010, but have never won the trophy!

Numbers weren't used on the back of players' shirts until the 1938 final – how did they tell who was who?

1

South Africa is the only World Cup host to be knocked out in the group stages of a World Cup final!

Uruguay striker Hector Castro accidentally cut off his right hand with an electric saw when he was just 13 years old working as a carpenter, but he still managed to score the winner in the 1930 World Cup final against Argentina!

6

World Cups have been won by the host nation six times, with the last being France in 1998!

17

Pele is the youngest ever World Cup winner, picking up a winners' medal in 1958 at just 17 years and 249 days old.

The Brazil legend is also the only player ever to win the World Cup three times – he did it in 1958, 1962 and 1970!

40

Way up the other end of the scale is former Italian goalkeeper Dino Zoff, who in 1982 became the oldest player to lift the trophy at 40 years and 133 days.

Wilfried Hannes and Holger Hieronymus were both picked for West Germany's 1982 World Cup squad, even though they could only see out of one eye!

Chelsea legend Gianfranco Zola is the only player to be sent off in a World Cup final – on his birthday! The Italian received a red in their second-round victory against Nigeria on his 28th birthday.

Sergio Batista (1986) and Gennaro Gattuso (2006) are apparently the only two players to have won the World Cup while sporting a full beard.

Lusail, the city that will host the opening game and final of the Qatar 2022 World Cup, doesn't even exist yet!

5

Bora Milutinovic is the only man to coach five different countries at the World Cup. The Serb coached Mexico (1986), Costa Rica (1990), the USA (1994), Nigeria (1998) and China (2002)!

6

England striker Gary Lineker won the Golden Boot award at the 1986 World Cup after scoring six goals. England reached the quarter-finals before losing to Diego Maradona's infamous 'Hand Of God' goal.

13

France's Just Fontaine holds the record for scoring the most goals in a single tournament – he scored 13 in 1958!

171

The 1998 World Cup was a proper goal-fest, with 171 goals being scored – it's the most tournament goals ever!

15

The longest surname in World Cup history is 15 letters long! Lefter Kucukandonyadis scored twice for Turkey at the 1954 tournament!

Scotland have qualified for the World Cup finals eight times – and have been knocked out in the first round eight times. Ouch!

3

England hero Sir Geoff Hurst is the only player to score a hat-trick in a World Cup final! The Three Lions legend hit his awesome treble as England beat West Germany 4–2 in the 1966 World Cup final!

16

The fastest World Cup goal by a substitute was scored by Denmark's Ebbe Sand against Nigeria in 1998 after just 16 seconds!

0

England have never won a World Cup penalty shoot-out, having lost on spot-kicks in 1990, 1998 and 2006!

17

Bulgaria went 17 games at World Cup finals without winning between 1962 and 1994, but ended the run in style with a 4–0 hammering of Greece in 1994!

2

South Africa defender Pierre Issa scored two own goals in his country's 3–0 defeat to hosts France at the 1998 World Cup!

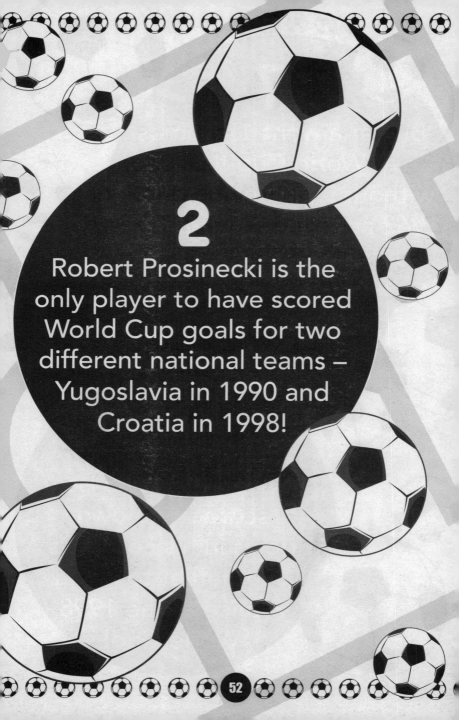

2

Robert Prosinecki is the only player to have scored World Cup goals for two different national teams – Yugoslavia in 1990 and Croatia in 1998!

Forget about Messi – if you want to talk about goalscorers, check out Fernando Peyroteo. The Portuguese striker boasts the world's greatest scoring ratio of 1.77 goals per game, having found the net an incredible 331 times in just 187 games for Sporting Lisbon between 1937 and 1949. Better still, he scored 4 or more goals in a game more than 30 times, including a phenomenal nine in one game!

357

Top-flight keepers must have dreaded facing Jimmy Greaves! The former Chelsea, Tottenham and West Ham goal machine scored a sensational 357 goals in the First Division between 1957 and 1970, which is a top-flight record in England!

260

Ex-Newcastle and Blackburn striker Alan Shearer might have hung up his boots back in 2006, but he's still the Premier League's record goalscorer. The powerhouse hitman scored an amazing 260 goals between 1992 and 2006, with his first coming for Blackburn against Crystal Palace and his last for Newcastle against Sunderland from the penalty spot in 2006!

35

Shearer also holds the record for the most goals in a Premier League season. The striker scored 35 goals in 42 games for Blackburn during the 1994–95 season, which fired Rovers to the title!

The record number of goals scored by one player in a single match is 16! French striker Stephan Stanis netted the incredible total while playing for Racing Club de Lens in December 1942.

31

The record number of goals for the 20-team, 38-game Premier League season is jointly held by Alan Shearer, Cristiano Ronaldo and Luis Suarez. They all hit 31 goals in 38 games!

60

But that's nothing compared to the record for the number of goals in an English season. That belongs to Bill 'Dixie' Dean, who scored 60 goals for Everton in 1927–28. Dean beat the previous record of 59 league goals, set the season before by Middlesbrough's George Camsell, by scoring SEVEN times in the last two matches!

175

Arsenal legend Thierry Henry holds the record for the most goals for one Premier League club. The French ace netted 175 goals for Arsenal between 1998 and 2007!

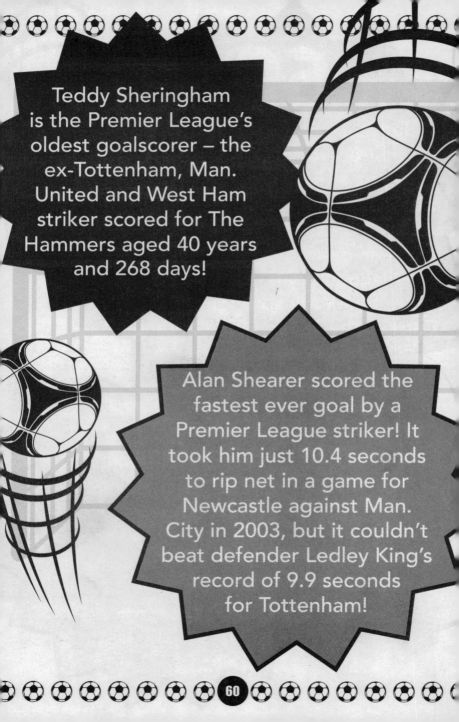

Teddy Sheringham is the Premier League's oldest goalscorer – the ex-Tottenham, Man. United and West Ham striker scored for The Hammers aged 40 years and 268 days!

Alan Shearer scored the fastest ever goal by a Premier League striker! It took him just 10.4 seconds to rip net in a game for Newcastle against Man. City in 2003, but it couldn't beat defender Ledley King's record of 9.9 seconds for Tottenham!

7

Wales legend Craig Bellamy has scored for seven different Premier League clubs, which is a record! Bellers bagged for Coventry, Liverpool, Blackburn, Newcastle, West Ham, Man. City and Cardiff – phew!

516

Emile Heskey is a legend, and he's also the striker with the most Prem appearances! The ex-England ace played 516 Prem games for Leicester, Liverpool, Birmingham, Wigan and Aston Villa!

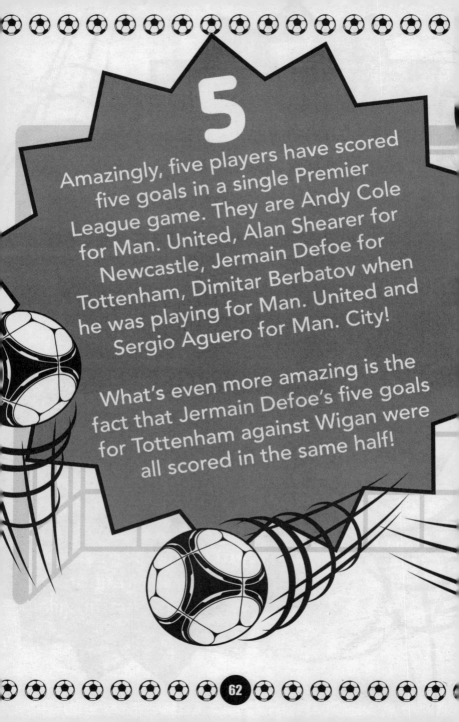

5

Amazingly, five players have scored five goals in a single Premier League game. They are Andy Cole for Man. United, Alan Shearer for Newcastle, Jermain Defoe for Tottenham, Dimitar Berbatov when he was playing for Man. United and Sergio Aguero for Man. City!

What's even more amazing is the fact that Jermain Defoe's five goals for Tottenham against Wigan were all scored in the same half!

11

Leicester striker Jamie Vardy holds the record for scoring in the most consecutive Premier League games. The speedy striker netted in 11 games on the trot, beating former Manchester United star Ruud van Nistelrooy's previous record of ten – against Manchester United!

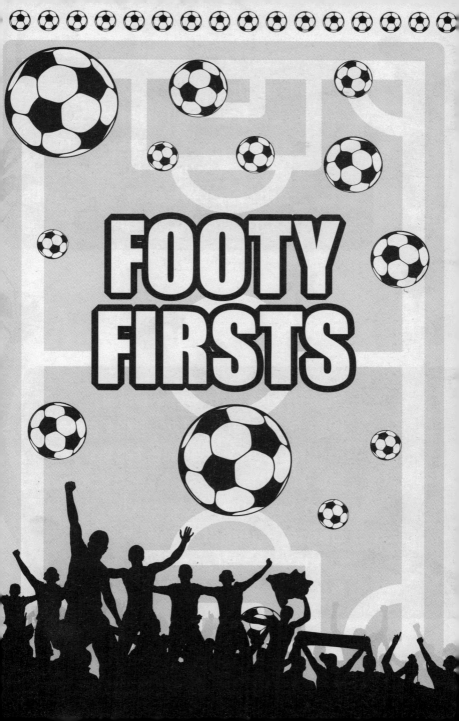

FOOTY FIRSTS

The first live coverage of a football match was shown on television in 1937. It was a practice match played at Arsenal's Highbury stadium.

Sheffield United's Brian Deane scored the first goal in Premier League history! He bagged just five minutes into Sheffield United's game against Manchester United at Bramall Lane on August 15, 1992.

In 2003–04 Arsenal became the first (and only) team to go the whole season unbeaten, earning the label 'The Invincibles'.

The first Sky television rights agreement was worth £304 million over five years – it's now worth a crazy £5.14 billion over three!

Footy superstar Alexis Sanchez was the first ever Chilean to play for Barcelona, and for Arsenal as well. Weird, huh?

French genius Eric Cantona scored the Premier League's first ever hat-trick in a 5–0 win for Leeds United against Tottenham Hotspur in August 1992.

The first televised Premier League goal was scored by Teddy Sheringham, for Nottingham Forest against Liverpool in August 1992!

The first player to reach 100 Premier League goals was Alan Shearer.

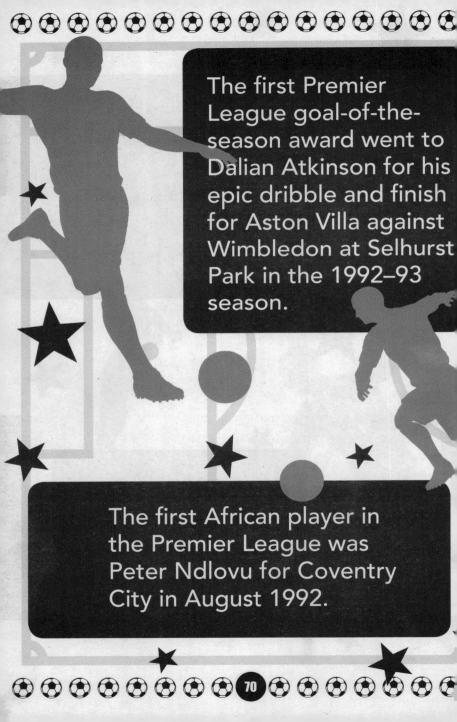

The first Premier League goal-of-the-season award went to Dalian Atkinson for his epic dribble and finish for Aston Villa against Wimbledon at Selhurst Park in the 1992–93 season.

The first African player in the Premier League was Peter Ndlovu for Coventry City in August 1992.

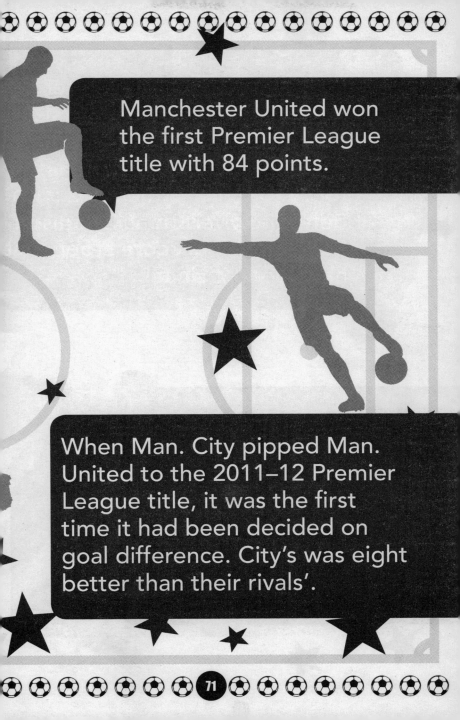

Manchester United won the first Premier League title with 84 points.

When Man. City pipped Man. United to the 2011–12 Premier League title, it was the first time it had been decided on goal difference. City's was eight better than their rivals'.

On October 20, 2001, Peter Schmeichel became the first goalkeeper to score in the Premier League when he netted for Aston Villa in their 3–2 defeat to Everton at Goodison Park. Only four more stoppers have done it since!

Chelsea was the first team to score more than 100 Premier League goals in a season as they smashed in 103 on their way to winning the title in 2009–10.

You might never have heard of Dennis Clarke, but he's a big deal in football history. The West Brom player became the first ever substitute to be used when he replaced John Kaye in the 1968 FA Cup final, which The Baggies won 1–0.

Welsh wizard Robert Earnshaw is the first, and so far only, player to score hat-tricks in the Premier League, Championship, League One, League Two, the FA Cup, League Cup and for his country. What a legend!

The first time goal nets were used in British football was way back in 1891!

The first time floodlights were used in English football was in November 1955, when Carlisle United faced Darlington in an FA Cup second-round replay.

Trevor Francis became the first £1 million transfer between English clubs when he joined Nottingham Forest from Birmingham City in 1979 for £1,150,000, which more than doubled the previous record!

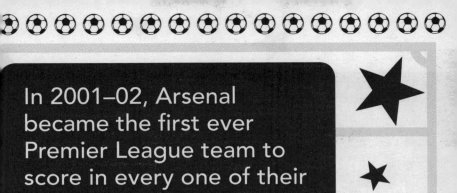

In 2001–02, Arsenal became the first ever Premier League team to score in every one of their 38 games!

White footballs were first introduced to English football in 1951!

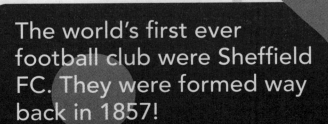

The world's first ever football club were Sheffield FC. They were formed way back in 1857!

The 1984 European Cup final was the first to be decided by a penalty shoot-out. Liverpool beat Roma 4–2 on spot-kicks after the match had finished 1–1 after extra-time!

The first ever goal in the European Cup was scored by Sporting Lisbon midfielder Joao Martins against Partizan Belgrade in September 1955!

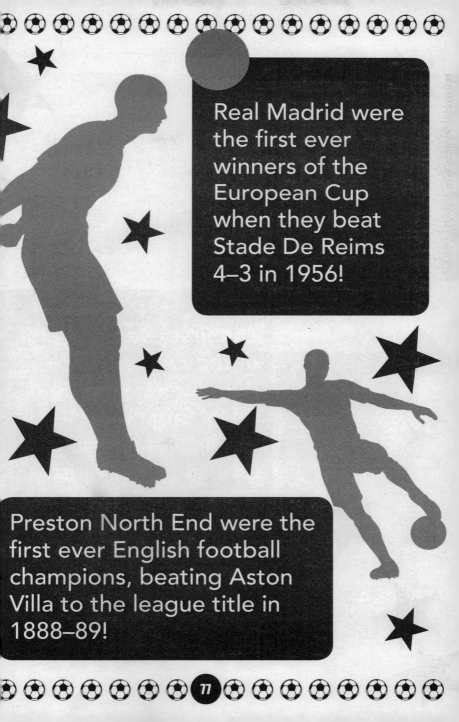

Real Madrid were the first ever winners of the European Cup when they beat Stade De Reims 4–3 in 1956!

Preston North End were the first ever English football champions, beating Aston Villa to the league title in 1888–89!

The first ever winners of the FA Cup were Wanderers, who beat Royal Engineers 1–0 in the final at Kennington Oval in front of just 2,000 spectators!

4

Dundee United have played Barcelona four times in professional fixtures and won all four, giving them a 100% win record against the Spanish giants!

1

There is only one team out of the four divisions in England and the four divisions in Scotland that have a 'J' in their name. It's St Johnstone.

Arsene Wenger has an asteroid named after him called 33179 Arsenewenger.

AC Milan is one of the most famous football clubs in the world, but it was actually founded as a cricket team!

Sweden international Stefan Schwarz arguably had the most bizarre clause to have ever been inserted into a player's contract. When signing for Sunderland in 1999, the Swede was banned from travelling into space!

VfL Wolfsburg once had a manager named Wolfgang Wolf.

29

The Scottish Cup tie between Falkirk and Inverness Caledonian Thistle in 1979 was postponed no fewer than 29 times because of bad weather!

869

The difference in Lionel Messi's age and Cristiano Ronaldo's age is 869 days, which is exactly the same difference as between Messi's son and Ronaldo's son!

0

Zinedine Zidane was never caught offside in his whole career.

Chelsea have been relegated more times than they've won the English league, with five league titles and six relegations!

27

Worldwide, there are 27 professional football clubs that take a Beatles song as their nickname – Villarreal in Spain being the most famous (The Yellow Submarines).

Neil Armstrong originally wanted to take a football to the moon – but NASA thought it was un-American and didn't let him!

The ball used in professional football has remained exactly the same size and shape for 120 years – 28 inches in circumference.

The first black-and-white jersey that Juventus wore was a Notts County kit that was brought in by an importer. It has become a tradition since then.

Former Hammer Alvin Martin achieved quite a feat in 1986 when he scored a hat-trick – against three different goalkeepers. He first scored past Newcastle goalkeeper Martin Thomas, who then came off at half-time with injury. With no substitute keeper, centre-back Chris Hedworth went between the sticks and was beaten for Martin's second before picking up an injury, at which point Geordie legend Peter Beardsley donned the gloves, being beaten for Martin's third. Not bad for a centre-back!

Sir Arthur Conan Doyle, the author of the Sherlock Holmes series, played keeper for Portsmouth under the name AC Smith.

2

Nottingham Forest are the only team to have won the European Cup more times than they've won their domestic league! They've only won one First Division title, but have lifted the European Cup twice!

Sheffield Wednesday were originally formed by a cricket team who played their games on a Wednesday!

Preston won the first ever English league title without losing a single match, and the FA Cup without conceding a goal in 1888–89!

The oldest football club in the world is Sheffield FC, who were formed in 1857. Notts County, formed in 1864, are the oldest league club!

The largest victory ever in an international soccer match was by Australia, when they beat American Samoa 32–0 in 2001. Archie Thompson scored a record 13 goals.

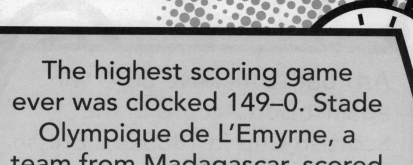

The highest scoring game ever was clocked 149–0. Stade Olympique de L'Emyrne, a team from Madagascar, scored 149 own goals. They did it to protest about the rubbish referee they'd had in the previous game!

But that's nothing compared to the smallest ever attendance in English football. Only 13 – yep, 13 – people turned up to watch Stockport County play Leicester City on May 7, 1921 for a Division Two game!

Arbroath's massive 36–0 win against Bon Accord in the Scottish Cup in 1885 is a British record, but did you know that on the same day Dundee Harp beat Aberdeen Rovers 35–0?

The former captain of the Qatar national team, Jafal Rashed Al-Kurawi, is believed to be the shortest footballer of all time. The tiny ex-Al Saad midfielder was 5ft 1in tall!

William 'Fatty' Foulke is thought to be the largest player ever! The Sheffield United, Chelsea, Bradford and England keeper could have weighed as much as 24 stone!

In the 1983–84 season in Romania's third division, which had 16 teams, there were just ten points difference between champions Muresul Deva (38 points), and bottom placed Minerul Aninoasa (28).

Perhaps even more astounding, however, is that the champions really were runaway leaders: second-placed UMT Timisoara mustered just 31 points, meaning that just two points separated second from fifteenth, who had 29 points. Truly unbelievable stuff – the final league table was outstanding!

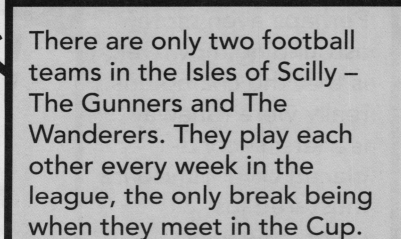

There are only two football teams in the Isles of Scilly – The Gunners and The Wanderers. They play each other every week in the league, the only break being when they meet in the Cup.

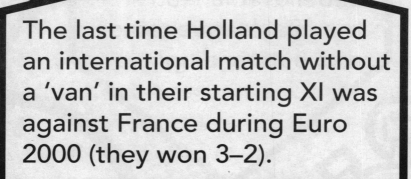

The last time Holland played an international match without a 'van' in their starting XI was against France during Euro 2000 (they won 3–2).

However, the last time they didn't have a 'van' in their entire match day squad (Peter van Vossen appeared as a late substitute against France) was way back in 1996 in a friendly 2–0 victory against China.

Andy Selva holds the distinction of being the only man to ever score a winning goal for San Marino, having scored in their 1–0 victory against Liechtenstein in 2004 (in 121 games, San Marino's record is 1 win, 3 draws and 117 losses).

Selva is also San Marino's all-time top goalscorer, with eight goals in 64 appearances. Manuel Marani is the only other man to score on more than one occasion for San Marino, with two goals in 34 appearances.

The powerhouse nations of Algeria, Ghana, South Korea and Saudi Arabia are part of an elite group, being the only countries in the world to boast an undefeated record against England.

Spanish striker Fernando Torres scored in seven official club competitions during the 2012–13 season. The Chelsea striker netted in the Premier League, Champions League, Europa League, FIFA Club World Cup, FA Community Shield, FA Cup and League Cup.

Jari Litmanen is widely considered to be Finland's greatest footballer. He made his Finland debut in 1989 (the 80s), was a regular throughout the 90s and 00s, before making his final appearance in 2011 (the 10s). No surprise then that he is the nation's most capped player, representing Finland a whopping 137 times.

Winning the Copa Libertadores with Atletico Mineiro has placed Ronaldinho in a very exclusive club, becoming one of only seven players to win both this and the UEFA Champions League, along with Cafu, Dida, Roque Junior, Carlos Tevez, Juan Pablo Sorin and Walter Samuel.

Falkirk and River Plate are the only two football clubs apart from Italy, England and Spain to have broken the world record transfer fee. Sydney Puddlefoot joined the Scottish side for a then record £5,000 in 1922. Argentina splashed out a record £23,000 on Bernabe Ferreyra ten years later.

The first English team to win a European trophy were West Auckland Town FC. They won the Sir Thomas Lipton trophy, one of football's first European competitions, in 1909 and 1911.

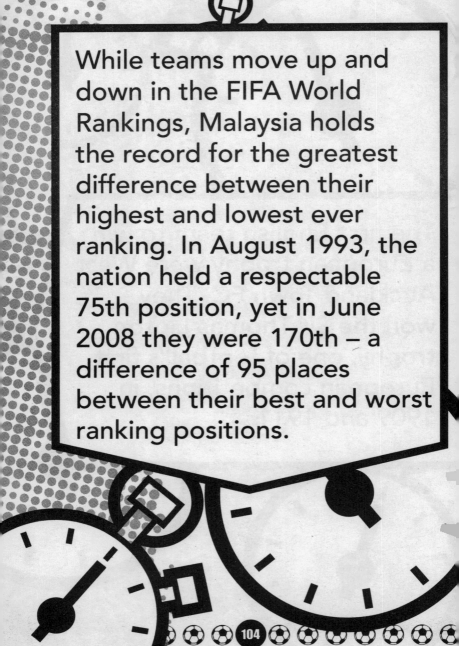

While teams move up and down in the FIFA World Rankings, Malaysia holds the record for the greatest difference between their highest and lowest ever ranking. In August 1993, the nation held a respectable 75th position, yet in June 2008 they were 170th – a difference of 95 places between their best and worst ranking positions.

BONKERS INJURIES

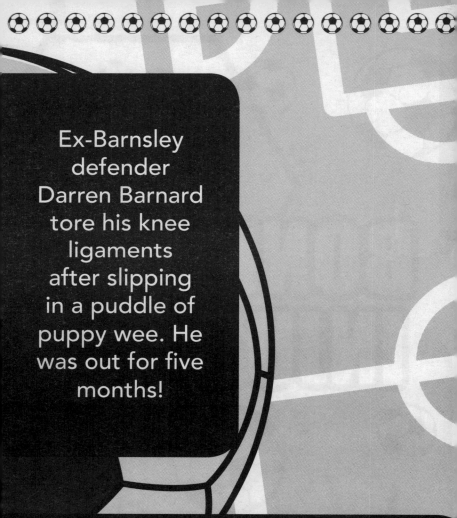

Ex-Barnsley defender Darren Barnard tore his knee ligaments after slipping in a puddle of puppy wee. He was out for five months!

In 1975, Man. United goalkeeper Alex Stepney dislocated his jaw by shouting at his defence!

When he was playing for Leeds, ex-England star Rio Ferdinand picked up an injury while watching TV! He had his foot up on a coffee table for ages and strained a tendon in his knee!

Former Wimbledon, Chelsea and Newcastle keeper Dave Beasant once dropped a bottle of salad cream in the kitchen and tried to breaks its fall with his bare foot. The bottle tore a tendon in his big toe and the stopper missed two months of the season!

Tough tackling midfielder David Batty was no stranger to picking up an injury or two during his playing days. Having endured a knee ligament problem, Batty suffered a setback when his two-year-old daughter ran over his ankle with her tricycle!

Alan Wright made a name for himself at Aston Villa, where he made more than 250 appearances. The 5ft 4ins left-back Wright once bought himself a Ferrari and managed to sprain his knee reaching for the accelerator pedal! He ended up swapping the sports car for a Rover 416.

Ahead of the 1990 World Cup, England captain Bryan Robson was given the unwanted challenge of trying to get Paul Gascoigne, who was fast asleep, out of his bed. After he picked the bed up and tipped Gazza out, he then dropped it on his toe and broke it!

Former Stoke midfielder Liam Lawrence once tripped over his dog during the night and fell down the stairs, putting himself out of action for a few weeks!

When at Sunderland, Kevin Kyle was forced to make a trip to hospital after his eight-month-old son kicked a bowl of hot water on to his lap!

Former Leicester, Spurs and USA star Kasey Keller knocked out his front teeth while pulling his golf clubs from the boot of his car!

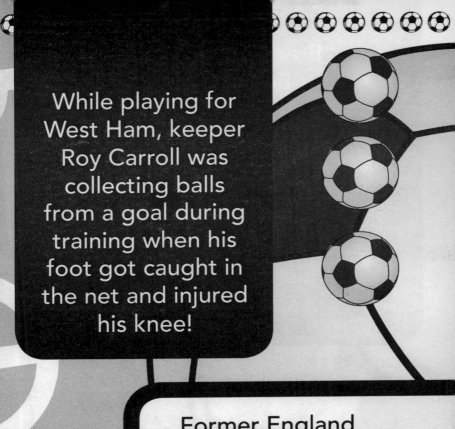

While playing for West Ham, keeper Roy Carroll was collecting balls from a goal during training when his foot got caught in the net and injured his knee!

Former England goalkeeper David James once pulled a muscle in his back when reaching for the television remote control!

Brentford goalkeeper
Chic Brodie's career came
to an end in October 1970 when
he collided with a sheepdog that
had run on to the pitch. Brodie
shattered his kneecap while the
dog got the ball. 'The dog might
have been a small one, but it
just happened to be
a solid one,' he said.

Norway defender Svein
Grondalen had to pull out of an
international during the 1970s
after colliding with a moose
while out jogging!

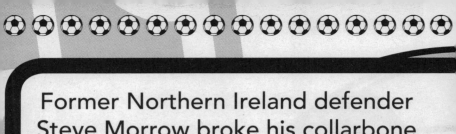

Former Northern Ireland defender Steve Morrow broke his collarbone after falling off the shoulders of Tony Adams while celebrating the 1993 League Cup final win against Sheffield Wednesday!

Alan Mullery missed England's 1964 tour of South America after injuring his back while brushing his teeth!

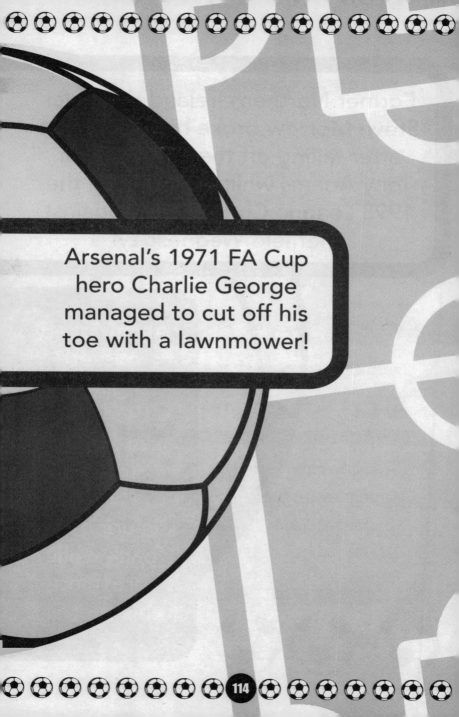

Arsenal's 1971 FA Cup hero Charlie George managed to cut off his toe with a lawnmower!

I'm A Celebrity . . . star and former England midfielder Kieron Dyer hurt his left eye when he ran into a pole in training for Newcastle, ruling him out for two weeks.

Ex-England Under–21 international Leroy Lita damaged a muscle while stretching after he woke up.

Liverpool reserve keeper Michael Stensgaard was forced to retire after suffering an injury to his shoulder while he attempted to fold down an ironing board!

Legendary Arsenal and England keeper David Seaman pulled a muscle as he tried to record *Coronation Street*, and also put his shoulder out trying to reel in a giant fish!

Argentinian Julio Arca was stung by a jellyfish when he went swimming in the sea during a Sunderland team training session. He broke out in a severe rash and was rushed to hospital!

All set to be West Germany's No.1 for the European Championships, Norbert Nigbur went out to celebrate with his fiancée. After the meal he tried to stand up and cried out in pain after tearing a cartilage in his knee. Harold Schumacher took over, and just to rub it in West Germany went and won the tournament!

After the Red Devils lost 2–0 to Arsenal in the FA Cup in 2003, Sir Alex Ferguson kicked a stray boot, which hit Becks and caused a cut just above the then England captain's eye!

Brazilian legend Ronaldo was left with a black eye after being struck by a microphone during a media scrum following his debut for Corinthians.

After scoring the winner against Chelsea in 2000, Arsenal star Thierry Henry went to celebrate in the corner of the pitch and needed treatment after hitting himself in the face with the corner flag!

Perry Groves was on the bench for an Arsenal match. They went one–nil up and he jumped up to celebrate only to hit his head on the roof of the dug-out! He knocked himself out and needed treatment from physio Gary Lewin.

Milan Rapaic once missed the start of Hajduk Split's season after sticking his boarding pass in his eye at the airport.

Allan Nielsen of Spurs missed several matches after his daughter poked him in the eye!

Shaun Goater injured a foot while playing for Man. City against Birmingham in 2003. He kicked an advertising hoarding while celebrating Nicolas Anelka's goal and had to be substituted!

Stalybridge Celtic keeper Mark Statham missed a game in 1999 after trapping his head in a car door!

Halifax defender Dave Robinson put his shoulder out falling off a kid's slide!

Man. City reserve keeper Richard Wright was ruled out of Everton's FA Cup fourth-round replay at Chelsea in 2006 after suffering a freak injury during the warm-up. Wright ignored a notice warning him not to practise in the goalmouth and promptly fell over the sign, suffering a twisted ankle.

13

Man. United hold the record for winning the most Premier League titles – they've lifted the trophy 13 times!

3

United also hold the record for the most consecutive title wins. They've won it three years on the trot on two separate occasions, from 1999–2001 and then again from 2007–09!

29

The record for the most Premier League wins in a season is held by Chelsea. They won 29 out of 38 games in 2004–05, and then did it again the following season!

1

Derby hold the record for the fewest wins in a Premier League season – they only won once during the 2007–08 season. They went down that season – weird, huh?

14

Arsenal hold the record for the most consecutive wins in the Premier League. The Gunners won 14 games on the trot between February 2002 and August 2002!

32

Poor old Derby have another Premier League record no one wants – they went 32 games without a win during the 2007–08 season. Ouch!

Ryan Giggs is the only Premier League player to score 100 goals without scoring a hat-trick.

13

Sir Alex Ferguson won 13 Premier League titles in his time in charge of Manchester United – that's more than any other manager!

The biggest Premier League defeat was Man. United's 9–0 victory over Ipswich in the 94–95 season!

260

Match Of The Day pundit Alan Shearer is the highest goalscorer in Premier League history – the England striker netted 260 goals for Blackburn and Newcastle between 1992 and 2006!

171

Chelsea legend Frank Lampard scored 171 Premier League goals – an unbelievable amount for a midfielder!

103

Chelsea scored a massive 103 goals on their way to winning the 2009–10 Premier League, which is still a record!

The Arsenal team of 2003–04 went the entire season unbeaten, winning 26 and drawing the other 12 of their 38 games on the way to winning the Prem. Preston didn't lose a game in the 1888–89 season either, with 18 wins and four draws!

100

Swindon conceded 100 goals in the 1993–94 season. Needless to say, they were relegated!

21

Man. United winger Ryan Giggs scored in every one of the first 21 Premier League seasons – what a legend!

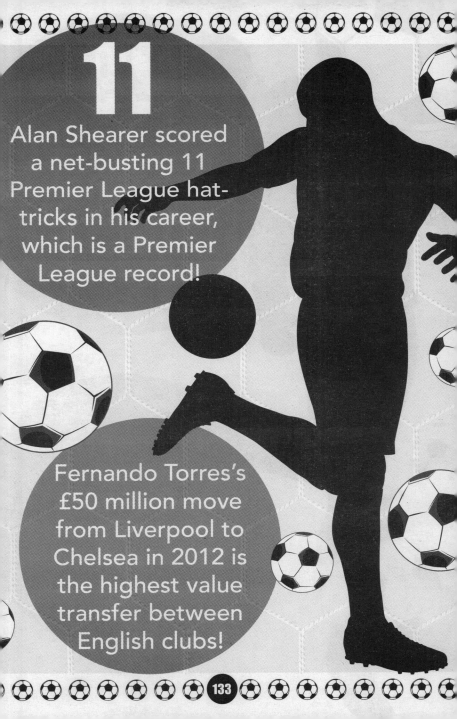

11

Alan Shearer scored a net-busting 11 Premier League hat-tricks in his career, which is a Premier League record!

Fernando Torres's £50 million move from Liverpool to Chelsea in 2012 is the highest value transfer between English clubs!

29

Chelsea have twice won 29 out of 38 Premier League games in a season – which is a Prem record! They achieved it in 2004–05 and 2005–06.

The highest Premier League attendance was when 76,398 fans turned up to watch Manchester United take on Blackburn in 2007!

32

Derby went an amazing 32 games without a win in the 2007–08 season.

10

Ex-Tottenham star Ledley King scored the fastest ever goal in Premier League history when he netted after just ten seconds into their game against Bradford at Valley Parade on December 9, 2000!

99

Kevin Davies and Lee Bowyer hold the unenviable record for the most yellow cards, with 99 bookings each!

When Chelsea won the Premier League in 2005, they ended up with a massive 95 points – a Prem record!

173

Liverpool, Aston Villa, West Ham, Man. City and Portsmouth goalkeeper David James kept 173 clean sheets during his Premier League career, which is a Prem record!

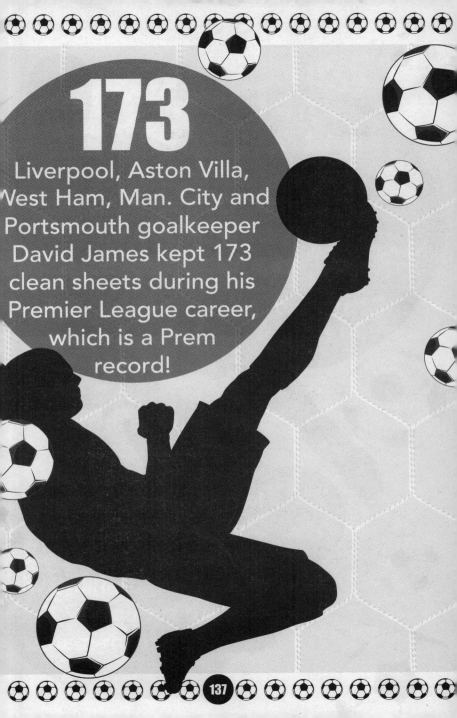

The earliest Premier League kick-off was on Sunday, October 2 in 2005, when Manchester City's game against Everton started at 11.15am.

127

Man. United legend Ryan Giggs holds the record for the most Premier League assists. In total, the wing wizard set up 127 goals for his team-mates!

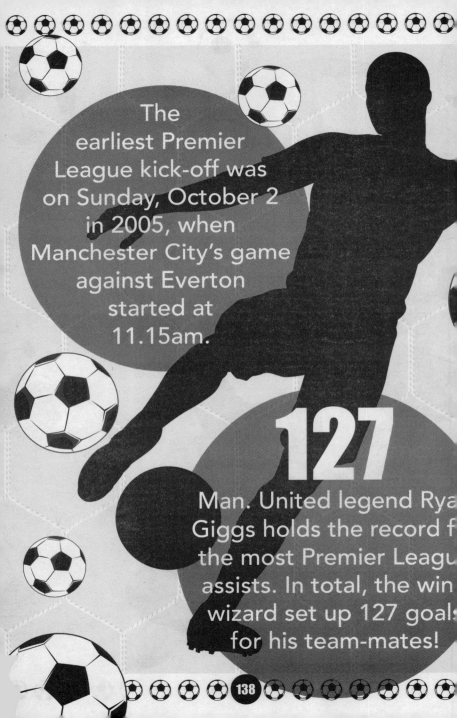

8

The record for the most red cards in the Premier League is held by Patrick Viera, Duncan Ferguson and Richard Dunne – all with eight!

47

When Bournemouth, Watford and Norwich played in the 2015–16 Premier League, it meant that 47 different teams had played in the Premier League since it started in 1992!

7

Only seven clubs have played in every Premier League season – Arsenal Aston Villa, Chelsea, Everton, Liverpool, Man. United and Tottenham!

5

Even more amazing is the fact that only five clubs have actually won the Premier League – Man. United, Blackburn, Arsenal, Chelsea and Man. City!

25

If you're the captain of a Premier League-winning side, you'll need big muscles to lift the trophy above your head – it weighs a massive 25kg, which is the same size as a fully grown bulldog!

14

The most goals in any top-flight game in the English league is a massive 14! Aston Villa beat Accrington 12–2 in 1892, while Tottenham won 10–4 against Everton in 1958.

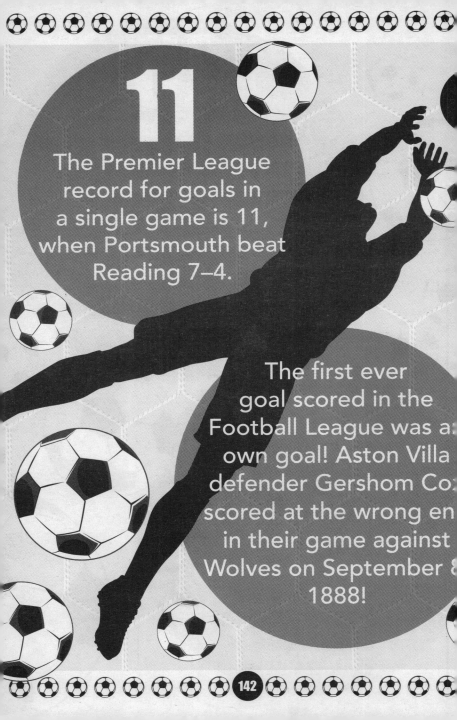

11

The Premier League record for goals in a single game is 11, when Portsmouth beat Reading 7–4.

The first ever goal scored in the Football League was an own goal! Aston Villa defender Gershom Cox scored at the wrong end in their game against Wolves on September 8 1888!

7

The record for the quickest top-flight goal in England goes to Preston's Bobby Langton – the winger scored after just seven seconds against Man. City on August 25, 1948.

When Bobby Langdon scored his record-breaking goal, Man. City keeper Frank Swift was still bending over to put his cap into the net!

31

It must have been tough being a Stoke fan in 1984–85. The team lost 31 out of their 42 matches in the First Division, which is a top-flight record!

The record number of Premier League defeats in one season is 29 – it's a record shared by the Ipswich side from 1994–95, Sunderland's 2005–06 team and Derby's 2007–08 flops!

Sunderland's 9–1 win at Newcastle in 1908 is the biggest ever away win! Even more amazing is the fact that their last five goals came in the final eight minutes!

Newcastle's 0–0 draw at home to Portsmouth in 1931 is the only league match in which neither side won a corner!

23

If you want help sleeping, you should have been a Norwich fan in 1978–79! The Canaries ground out 23 draws from their 42 league games! Zzzzzzz!

28

Ex-England keeper Ray Clemence holds the record for the most clean sheets in a top-flight season. The awesome shot-stopper kept 28 shut-outs for Liverpool in 1978–79!

14

Edwin van der Sar will never forget the 2008–09 season. His quality saves meant Man. United kept 14 clean sheets in a row – an incredible 1,311 minutes of footy. That beat Petr Cech's previous best of ten clean sheets in a row in 2004–05!

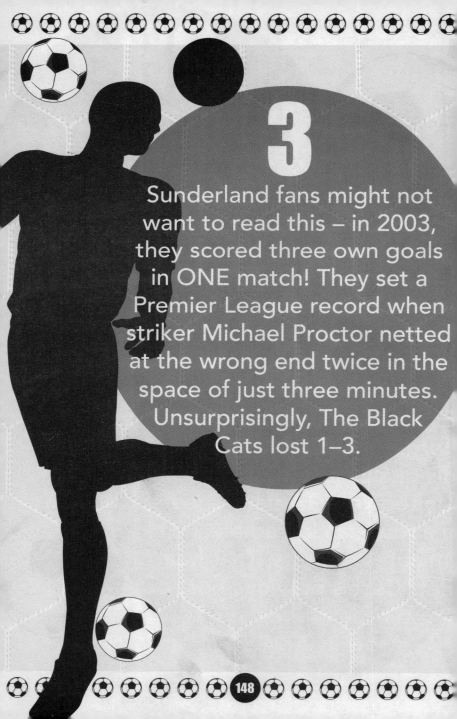

3

Sunderland fans might not want to read this – in 2003, they scored three own goals in ONE match! They set a Premier League record when striker Michael Proctor netted at the wrong end twice in the space of just three minutes. Unsurprisingly, The Black Cats lost 1–3.

50

One of the greatest English footballers of all time, Sir Stanley Matthews, is the oldest player the English top flight has ever seen! 'The Wizard Of The Dribble' was 50 years and five days old when he played his last game for Stoke in February 1953.

43

John Burridge became the Premier League's oldest ever player when he turned out for Manchester City in goal against QPR in 1995, aged 43 years and 162 days!

Matthew Briggs's appearance for Fulham in 2007, aged 16 years and 65 days, makes him the Premier League's youngest ever player. But he isn't the youngest ever top-flight star – Sunderland's Derek Forster played against Leicester aged just 15 years and 185 days in 1964!

18

Man. United hold the record for the biggest Premier League-winning margin, when they beat second-placed Arsenal by a massive 18 points in 1999–2000!

The smallest title-winning margin belongs to Man. City in 2011–12. They finished level on points with rivals Man. United, but won the league because their goal difference was eight better!

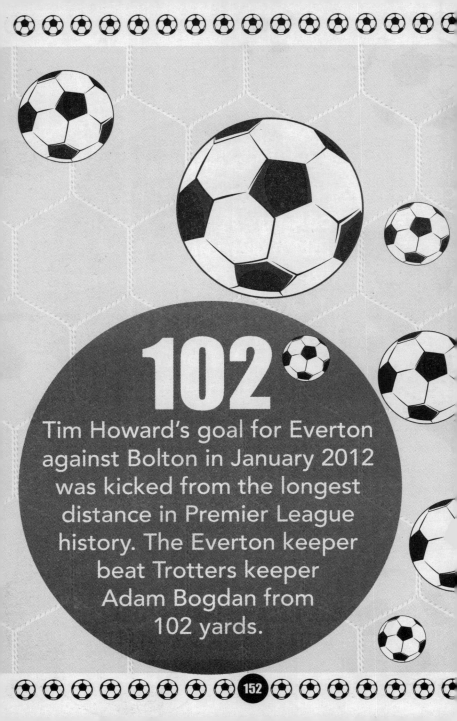

102

Tim Howard's goal for Everton against Bolton in January 2012 was kicked from the longest distance in Premier League history. The Everton keeper beat Trotters keeper Adam Bogdan from 102 yards.

310

USA keeper Brad Friedel holds the record for the most consecutive Premier League appearances. He played in every single match from August 2004 to October 2012, an amazing 310 games!

The most consecutive wins was 10 by Arsena (10 Feb 2002 to 24 Aug 2002).

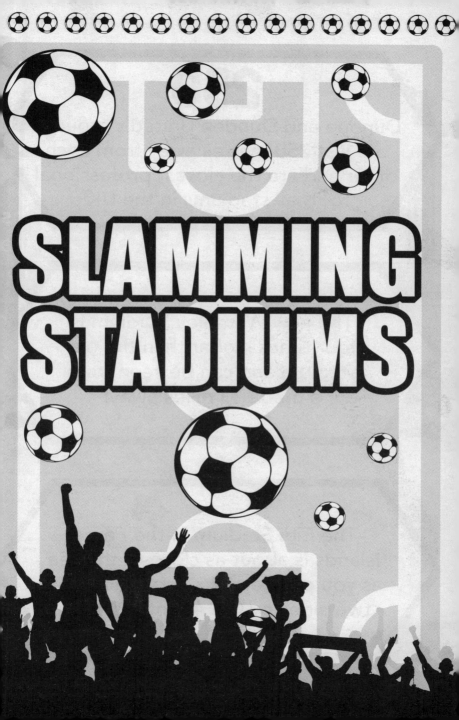

SLAMMING STADIUMS

250

Dundee and Dundee United's grounds are just 250 metres away from each other and are the closest professional football stadiums in the UK!

The new Wembley Stadium is four times higher than the old stadium and can be seen from a mega 13 miles away!

The Eidi Stadium in the Faroe Islands is about as close to the sea as you can get – it's surrounded on two sides by the Atlantic Ocean!

2,618

There are 2,618 toilets at Wembley – that's more than any other sports venue on the planet!

Sheffield United's Bramall Lane ground, opened in 1855, is the oldest major stadium in the world still hosting football matches!

The Allianz Arena in Munich, home to Bayern and 1860, has 1,056 illuminated panels on the outside which can be lit red, white and blue, depending on which team is playing at home that week!

120

It took 120 builders 13 months to build the original San Siro Stadium, which held just 35,000 fans!

The Premier League stadium with the biggest capacity is Manchester United's Old Trafford, which can hold 75,635 fans!

The stadium with the largest capacity in the world is the Rungrado May Day Stadium in North Korea, which can hold an incredible 150,000 fans!

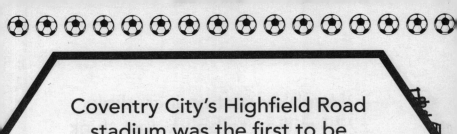

Coventry City's Highfield Road stadium was the first to be converted from standing terraces to an all-seater stadium in 1981!

Despite hosting home games for IBV, a top division club in Iceland, Hasteinvollur is situated just round the corner from a volcano! The views are said to be lava-ly!

256

There are a massive 256 floodlights covering each roof of the San Siro Stadium, each one using 3,500 watts of power!

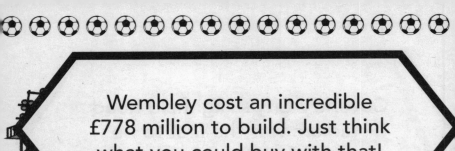

Wembley cost an incredible £778 million to build. Just think what you could buy with that!

The highest official attendance at a football match was recorded as 173,850 for the 1950 World Cup final between Brazil and Uruguay at the Maracana in Rio de Janeiro. However, some reckon the actual total was nearer to 200,000!

168

West Bromwich Albion's Hawthorns stadium is 168 metres above sea level, which makes it the highest ground in the UK!

3,637

But that's nothing compared to the Estadio Hernando Siles stadium in Bolivia – that's an eye-popping 3,637 metres above sea level!

At the other end of the scale, Grimsby Town's Blundell Park is the lowest ground in the UK at just 0.6 metres above sea level, while Southampton's St Mary's Stadium is just behind it at 0.9 metres!

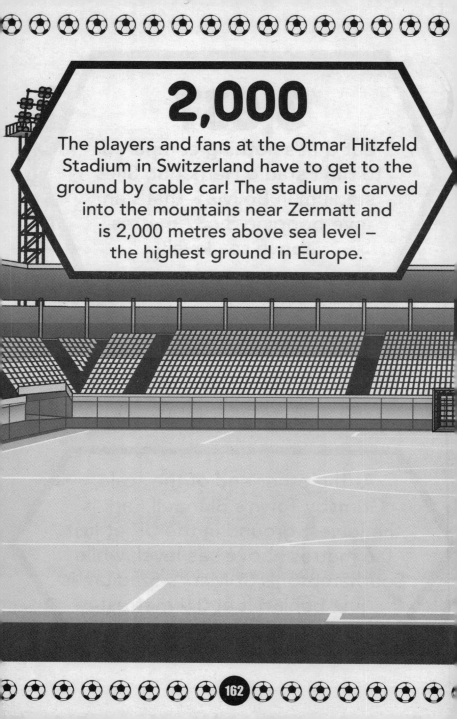

2,000

The players and fans at the Otmar Hitzfeld Stadium in Switzerland have to get to the ground by cable car! The stadium is carved into the mountains near Zermatt and is 2,000 metres above sea level – the highest ground in Europe.

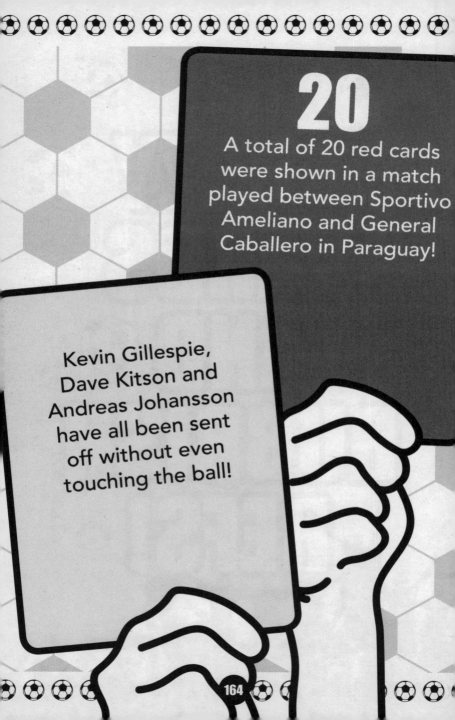

20

A total of 20 red cards were shown in a match played between Sportivo Ameliano and General Caballero in Paraguay!

Kevin Gillespie, Dave Kitson and Andreas Johansson have all been sent off without even touching the ball!

548
Javier Zanetti didn't get a red card in Serie A until his 548th match.

5
Newcastle striker Craig Bellamy set the record for the fastest Champions League red card when he was sent off just five minutes into their game with Inter Milan back in 2002!

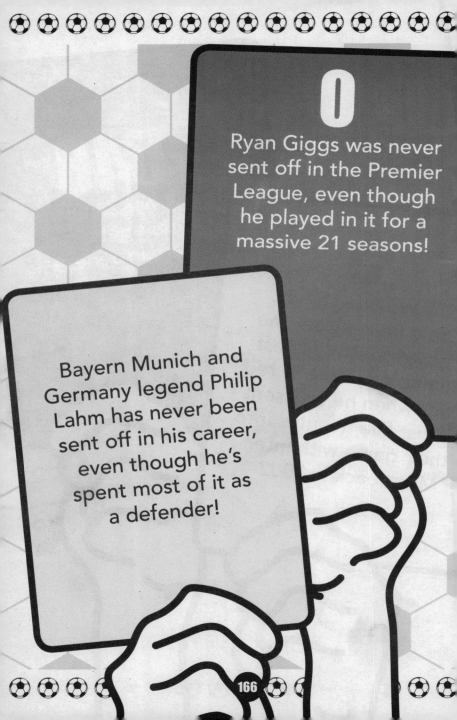

0

Ryan Giggs was never sent off in the Premier League, even though he played in it for a massive 21 seasons!

Bayern Munich and Germany legend Philip Lahm has never been sent off in his career, even though he's spent most of it as a defender!

English referee Graham Poll showed three yellow cards to a Croatian player before sending him off in their first round game against Australia at the 2006 FIFA World Cup! Josip Simunic was shown a yellow card by Poll in the 61st minute. In the 90th minute, Poll held up another yellow card in front of Simunic for another foul, but did not follow it with a red card. Finally, after he had blown the final whistle, Simunic pushed the referee, who showed him a third yellow and finally showed him the red!

In the space of five crazy minutes at Sunderland in November 1998, Barnsley striker Ashley Ward scored, missed a penalty and was sent off.

Match Of The Day presenter Gary Lineker was never booked in his entire footy career. Wow!

Yellow and red cards were invented by English referee Ken Aston, and introduced at the 1970 World Cup.

Referees only started using whistles in England in 1878. Before that, they used handkerchiefs to call for a stoppage in play!

The first ever player in the Football League to be sent off was David Wagstaffe, who was playing for Blackburn Rovers at Leyton Orient on October 2, 1976.

Referee Alf Bond, who took charge of the 1956 FA Cup final between Man. City and Birmingham only had one arm! He lost his right one in a rubber factory accident when he was 19 years old!

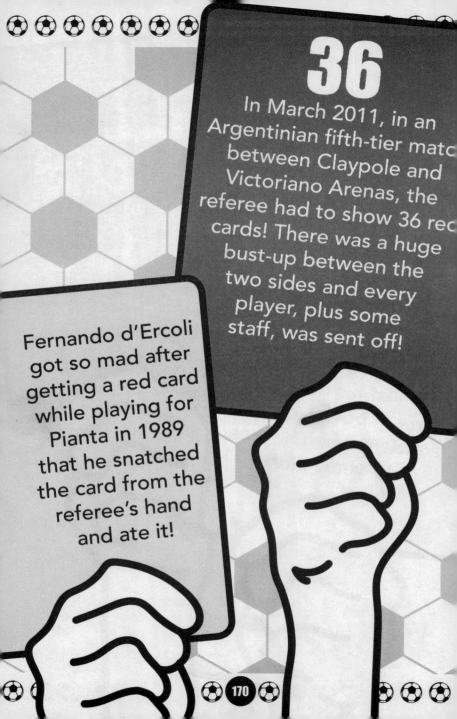

36

In March 2011, in an Argentinian fifth-tier match between Claypole and Victoriano Arenas, the referee had to show 36 red cards! There was a huge bust-up between the two sides and every player, plus some staff, was sent off!

Fernando d'Ercoli got so mad after getting a red card while playing for Pianta in 1989 that he snatched the card from the referee's hand and ate it!

Current BT Sport pundit and former Derby, Blackburn and Leicester midfielder Robbie Savage has gone into the referee's notebook more than any other player – he received a yellow card an amazing 89 times!

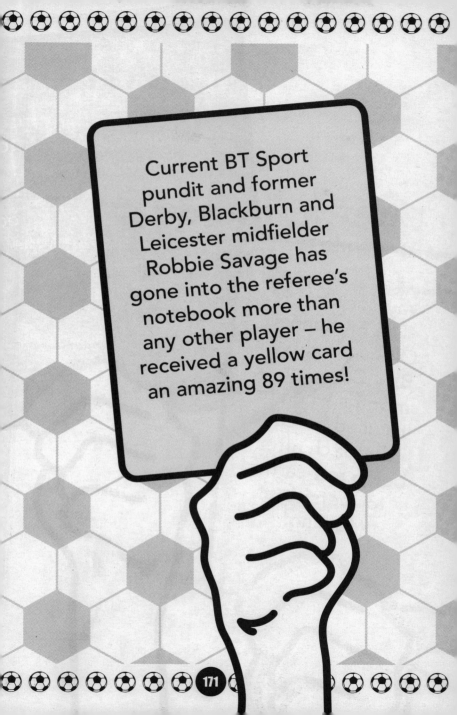

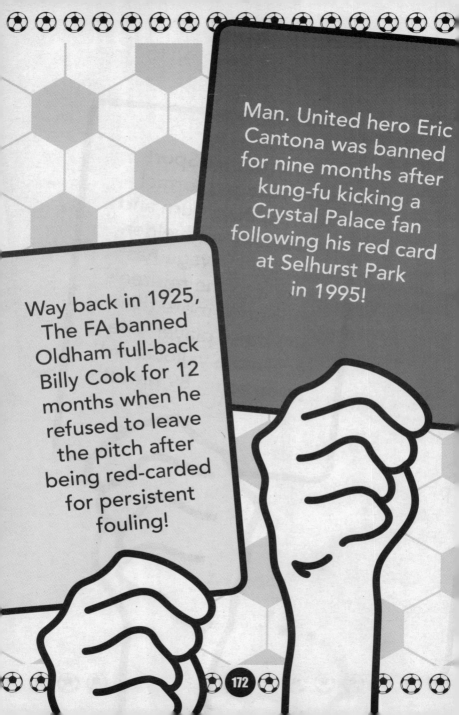

Man. United hero Eric Cantona was banned for nine months after kung-fu kicking a Crystal Palace fan following his red card at Selhurst Park in 1995!

Way back in 1925, The FA banned Oldham full-back Billy Cook for 12 months when he refused to leave the pitch after being red-carded for persistent fouling!

At the time of the first FA Cup and international fixtures, two umpires, one per team, were employed as officials – and each side had to appeal to them. The referee stood on the touchline and was only 'referred' to if the umpires couldn't agree.

Russian referee Valentin Ivanov went card crazy during a fiery World Cup battle in 2006 between Portugal and Holland! The last-16 clash saw four players sent off and another 12 yellow cards dished out. Portugal's Maniche scored the only goal of the game as both teams ended the game with nine men!

Welsh referee Clive Thomas broke Brazilian hearts by denying them a goal in their game against Sweden in the 1978 World Cup. With the score at 1–1, the South Americans thought they'd snatched a last-gasp winner when Zico headed home from a corner, but Thomas blew the final whistle a fraction of a second before the ball crossed the line and the goal didn't count!

On August 31, 1996, Wendy Toms became the first woman to referee a senior match in England when she took charge of the Conference fixture between Woking and Telford United!

62

It looks huge, but the Champions League trophy is smaller than the Premier League trophy! It stands at just 62cm tall and cost £6,000 to make!

You'd expect a trophy made of silver to be really heavy, but the Champions League trophy is really light. While the Prem trophy weighs 25kg, the Champions League weighs just 7.5kg!

6

The original European Cup was kept by Real Madrid after they won it for a sixth time in 1966. The design of the trophy hasn't changed since Celtic beat Inter Milan in 1967.

33,000

Only 33,000 fans saw Benfica's 3–2 win over Barcelona in the 1961 European Cup final at Switzerland's Wankdorf Stadium. It's the lowest ever for a European Cup final!

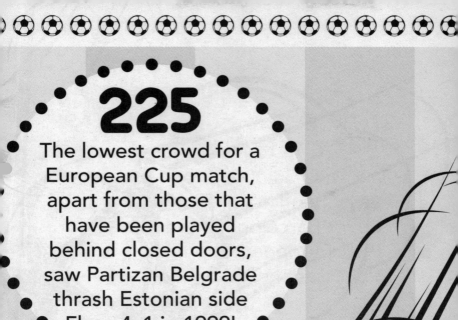

225

The lowest crowd for a European Cup match, apart from those that have been played behind closed doors, saw Partizan Belgrade thrash Estonian side Flora 4–1 in 1999!

13

Real Madrid hold the record for the most appearances in the European Cup final with 13, and have won ten of them!

16

When Arsenal reached the knockout stages of the Champions League in 2015–16, it was their 16th season in a row!

135,826

The 1970 European Cup semi-final second leg, between Celtic and Leeds, drew 135,826 fans – the biggest attendance in the competition's history. The huge crowd at Hampden Park saw Celtic win 2–1!

14

The record for the most goals in a European Cup match is 14, when Feyenoord beat KR Reykjavik 12–2 in the first round in 1969–70.

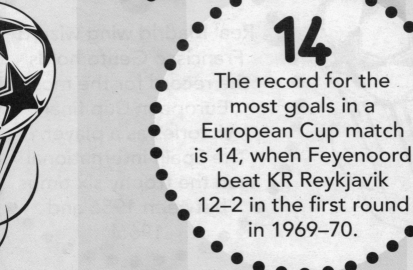

0

Brazil legend Ronaldo has never won the Champions League, despite playing for five teams that did. Zlatan Ibrahimovic hasn't ever won it either!

6

Real Madrid wing wizard Francisco Gento holds the record for the most European Cup final victories as a player. The Spain international won the trophy six times between 1956 and 1966!

3

Dutch legend Clarence Seedorf has won the Champions League with three different clubs: Ajax in 1995, Real Madrid in 1998 and AC Milan in 2003 and 2007!

10

Real Madrid's 7–3 win over Frankfurt at Hampden Park in 1960 is still the highest-scoring final ever!

The youngest player to score a Champions League hat-trick is Real Madrid legend Raul. The striker was just 18 years and 114 days old when he bagged a treble against Turkish side Fenerbahce!

10.2

Dutch striker Roy Makaay holds the record for the fastest ever goal in the tournament's history. It took the striker just 10.2 seconds to score for Bayern Munich against Real Madrid at the Allianz Arena in 2007!

141

Italy legend Paolo Maldini played a jaw-dropping 141 European Cup matches for AC Milan between 1988 and 2008 – that's a record in the competition!

7

Swansea ace Bafetimbi Gomis holds the record for the quickest Champions League hat-trick! The striker netted three times in just seven minutes for Lyon against Dinamo Zagreb on December 7, 2011.

5

When Man. United won the Champions League in 1999, they only won five of their 11 games! But they drew the other six, meaning they didn't lose a single game!

3

Only three clubs fielding teams made up entirely of players from that country have won the UEFA Champions League. They are Real Madrid in 1966, Celtic in 1967 and Steaua Bucharesti in 1986.

6

Barcelona reached the semi-finals six seasons in a row, from 2008 to 2013, which is a Champions League record!

4

Celtic are the only club to have the distinction of completing a quadruple in the same season, winning the Scottish league, both domestic cups and the European Cup in the 1966–67 season!

10

In 2006, Arsenal produced the best defensive effort ever in the history of the Champions League, going ten games without conceding a goal!

In 2015–16, Barcelona became the first team to have two players score ten or more goals in the same Champions League campaign when Lionel Messi and Neymar both hit ten!

6

After their defeat to Barcelona in the 2015 Champions League final, Juventus became the first side to lose in six finals!

Pedro only had one touch of the ball after coming on as a sub in the 2015 Champions League final against Juventus. But it wasn't a bad touch – he set up Neymar for the third and final goal!

0

Since the competition became the Champions League in 1992, no team has ever won the trophy two years in a row!

25

The record for the longest unbeaten run in the Champions League belongs to Manchester United. The Red Devils went 25 games without defeat between September 19, 2007 and May 27, 2009!

10

Real Madrid hold the record for the most Champions League wins with an incredible ten titles!

5

Real Madrid not only hold the record for the most European Cup wins, but also they're the only club to have won five times in a row! They won the first five years of the European Cup from 1956 to 1960!

17

Cristiano Ronaldo scored 17 goals in the 2014 Champions League, setting a record for the number of goals in a single tournament!

1

The 2014 Champions League final between Real Madrid and Atletico Madrid was the first time the final was between two clubs from the same city!

Despite seven attempts, Bayern Munich has never beaten a team led by Carlo Ancelotti in the Champions League!

Barcelona might be Euro kings right now, but they didn't win their first European Cup until 1992 when they beat Sampdoria 1–0 at Wembley!

3

Carlo Ancelotti is the only coach to win three Champions League titles, although Bob Paisley won three European Cups with Liverpool.

BIGGEST WORLD

1 Gareth Bale
Tottenham Hotspur to Real Madrid
£86 million

2 Cristiano Ronaldo
Man. United to Real Madrid
£80 million

3 Luis Suarez
Liverpool to Barcelona
£75 million

4 Neymar
Santos to Barcelona
£71.5 million

5 James Rodriguez
Monaco to Real Madrid
£63 million

TRANSFERS

6 **Angel Di Maria**
Real Madrid to Man. United
£59.7 million

7 **Zlatan Ibrahimovic**
Inter Milan to Barcelona
£59 million

8 **Kaka**
AC Milan to Real Madrid
£56 million

9 **Edinson Cavani**
Napoli to PSG
£55 million

10 **Kevin De Bruyne**
Wolfsburg to Man. City
£54 million

BIGGEST PREMIER

1 Angel Di Maria
Real Madrid to Man. United
£59.7 million

2 Kevin De Bruyne
Wolfsburg to Man. City
£54.5 million

3 Fernando Torres
Liverpool to Chelsea
£50 million

4 Raheem Sterling
Liverpool to Man. City
£49 million

5 Mesut Ozil
Real Madrid to Arsenal
£42.5 million

LEAGUE TRANSFERS

6 Sergio Aguero
Atletico Madrid to Man. City
£38 million

7 Juan Mata
Chelsea to Man. United
£37.1 million

8= Andy Carroll
Newcastle to Liverpool
£35 million

8= Alexis Sanchez
Barcelona to Arsenal
£35 million

10 Fernandinho
Shakhtar Donetsk to Man. City
£34 million

BIGGEST PREMIER

1 **Man. United 9–0 Ipswich**
March 4, 1995

2 **Spurs 9–1 Wigan**
November 22, 2009

3= **Chelsea 8–0 Wigan**
May 9, 2010

3= **Chelsea 8–0 Aston Villa**
December 23, 2012

3= **Newcastle 8–0 Sheffield Wednesday**
September 19, 1999

3= **Southampton 8–0 Sunderland**
October 18, 2014

7= **Nottingham Forest 1–8 Man. United**
February 6, 1999

EAGUE WINS

7= **Middlesbrough 8–1 Man. City**
May 11, 2008

9= **Blackburn 7–0 Forest**
November 18, 1995

9= **Arsenal 7–0 Everton**
May 11, 2005

9= **Arsenal 7–0 Middlesbrough**
January 14, 2006

9= **Man. United 7–0 Barnsley**
October 25, 1997

9= **Chelsea 7–0 Stoke**
April 25, 2010

9= **Man. City 7–0 Norwich**
November 2, 2013

MOST PREMIER LEAGUE APPEARANCES

1	Ryan Giggs	632
2	Frank Lampard	609
3	Gareth Barry	573
4	David James	572
5	Gary Speed	534
6	Emile Heskey	516
7	Rio Ferdinand	514
8	Mark Schwarzer	510
9	Jamie Carragher	508
10	Phil Neville	505

TOP TEN YOUNGEST PREMIER LEAGUE PLAYERS

1	Matthew Briggs	16 yrs	68 days
2	Izzy Brown	16 yrs	117 days
3	Aaron Lennon	16 yrs	128 days
4	Rushian Hepburn-Murphy	16 yrs	176 days
5	Jose Baxter	16 yrs	191 days
6	Gary McSheffrey	16 yrs	198 days
7	Reece Oxford	16 yrs	236 days
8	Jack Robinson	16 yrs	250 days
9	Jack Wilshere	16 yrs	255 days
10	Mark Platts	16 yrs	264 days

WORLD'S BIGGEST

1 **Rungrado May Day Stadium**
Pyongyang, North Korea
150,000

2 **Nou Camp**
Barcelona, Spain
99,786

3 **Azteca Stadium**
Mexico City, Mexico
95,500

4 **FNB Stadium**
Johnannesburg, South Africa
94,736

5 **The Rose Bowl**
Pasedena, USA
92,542

FOOTBALL STADIUMS

6 **Wembley Stadium**
London, England
90,000

7 **Gelora Bung Karno Stadium**
Jakarta, Indonesia
88,306

8 **Bukit Jalil National Stadium**
Kuala Lumpur, Malaysia
87,411

9 **Borg El Arab Stadium**
Alexandria, Egypt
86,000

0 **Azadi Stadium**
Tehran, Iran
84,412

TOP WORLD CUP GOALSCORERS

1 **Mirslav Klose** Germany 16

2 **Ronaldo** Brazil 15

3 **Gerd Muller** West Germany 14

4 **Just Fontaine** France 13

5 **Pele** Brazil 12

6= **Sandor Kocsis** Hungary 11

6= **Jurgen Klinsmann** Germany 11

8= **Helmut Rahn** West Germany 10

8= **Teofilo Cubillas** Peru 10

8= **Grzegorz Lato** Poland 10

8= **Gary Lineker** England 10

8= **Gabriel Batistuta** Argentina 10

8= **Thomas Muller** Germany 10

MOST INTERNATIONAL APPEARANCES

1	Ahmed Hassan	Egypt	184
2=	Mohamed Al-Deayea	Saudi Arabia	178
2=	Claudio Suarez	Mexico	178
4	Hossam Hassan	Egypt	169
5=	Ivan Hurtado	Ecuador	167
5=	Vitalijs Astafjevs	Latvia	167
7=	Cobi Jones	USA	164
7=	Adnan Al-Talyani	UAE	164
9	Sami Al-Jaber	Saudi Arabia	163
10	Martin Reim	Estonia	157

ENGLAND'S BIGGEST

1	**Wembley Stadium**	England	90,000
2	**Old Trafford**	Man. United	75,653
3	**Emirates**	Arsenal	60,260
4	**Etihad Stadium**	Man. City	55,097
5	**St James' Park**	Newcastle United	52,338

FOOTBALL GROUNDS

6 **Stadium Of Light**
Sunderland   48,707

7 **Anfield**
Liverpool   44,742

8 **Villa Park**
Aston Villa   42,660

9 **Stamford Bridge**
Chelsea   41,798

10 **Hillsborough**
Sheffield Wednesday   39,732

THE UK'S BIGGEST

1 **Wembley Stadium**
England   90,000

2 **Old Trafford**
Man. United   75,653

3 **Millennium Stadium**
Wales   74,500

4 **Celtic Park**
Celtic   60,411

5 **Emirates Stadium**
Arsenal   60,260

FOOTBALL GROUNDS

6 **Etihad Stadium**
Man. City   55,097

7 **St James' Park**
Newcastle United   52,338

8 **Hampden Park**
Scotland   51,866

9 **Ibrox**
Rangers   50,947

10 **Stadium Of Light**
Sunderland   48,707

TOP TEN ENGLISH LEAGUE WINNERS

1	**Manchester United**	**20**
2	**Liverpool**	**18**
3	**Arsenal**	**13**
4	**Everton**	**9**
5	**Aston Villa**	**7**
6	**Sunderland**	**6**
7	**Chelsea**	**5**
8=	**Manchester City**	**4**
8=	**Newcastle United**	**4**
8=	**Sheffield Wednesday**	**4**

MOST FA CUP WINS

1	**Arsenal**	**12**
2	**Manchester United**	**11**
3	**Tottenham Hotspur**	**8**
4=	**Liverpool**	**7**
4=	**Chelsea**	**7**
4=	**Aston Villa**	**7**
7=	**Newcastle United**	**6**
7=	**Blackburn Rovers**	**6**
9=	**Everton**	**5**
9=	**West Bromwich Albion**	**5**
9=	**Manchester City**	**5**
9=	**Wanderers**	**5**

TOP 10 YOUNGEST PREMIER

1 James Vaughan | Apr 10, 2005
Everton v Cryst. Palace | 16 years 270 days

2 James Milner | Dec 26, 2002
Leeds v Sunderland | 16 years 356 days

3 Wayne Rooney | Oct 19, 2002
Everton v Arsenal | 16 years 360 days

4 Cesc Fabregas | Aug 25, 2004
Arsenal v Blackburn | 17 years 113 days

5 Michael Owen | May 6, 1997
Liverpool v Wimbledon | 17 years 132 days

LEAGUE GOALSCORERS

6 Andy Turner   Sep 5, 1992
Tottenham v Everton   17 years, 166 days

7 Federico Macheda   Apr 5, 2009
Man. Utd v Aston Villa   17 years 226 days

8 Raheem Sterling   Oct 20, 2012
Liverpool v Reading   17 years 312 days

9 Mikael Forssell   Feb 20, 1999
Chelsea v Nott. Forest   17 years 342 days

10 Danny Cadamarteri   Sep 20, 1997
Everton v Barnsley   17 years 343 days

MOST EUROPEAN CUP WINS

1	**Real Madrid**	Spain	10
2	**AC Milan**	Italy	7
3=	**Bayern Munich**	Germany	5
3=	**Barcelona**	Spain	5
3=	**Liverpool**	England	5
6	**Ajax**	Holland	4
7=	**Inter Milan**	Italy	3
7=	**Manchester United**	England	3
9=	**Juventus**	Italy	2
9=	**Benfica**	Portugal	2
9=	**Nottingham Forest**	England	2
9=	**Porto**	Portugal	2

THE FA CUP

0

Leicester City have reached four FA Cup finals, in 1949, 1961, 1963 and 1969, but haven't won any of them.

12

Arsenal hold the record for the number of FA Cup wins with 12! Manchester United are hot on their heels with 11 wins!

43

A massive 43 different clubs have won the FA Cup since it was first played way back in 1872!

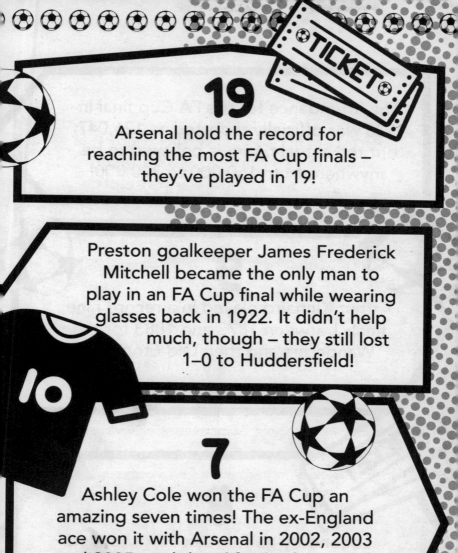

19

Arsenal hold the record for reaching the most FA Cup finals – they've played in 19!

Preston goalkeeper James Frederick Mitchell became the only man to play in an FA Cup final while wearing glasses back in 1922. It didn't help much, though – they still lost 1–0 to Huddersfield!

7

Ashley Cole won the FA Cup an amazing seven times! The ex-England ace won it with Arsenal in 2002, 2003 and 2005, and then lifted it four more times with Chelsea, in 2007, 2009, 2010 and 2012!

The attendance for the FA Cup final in 1923 was officially reported as 126,047, but the actual figure is believed to be anywhere from 150,000 to 300,000!

9

Arthur Kinnaird played in a record nine finals between 1873 and 1883 for the Wanderers and then Old Etonians.

TICKET

8

Legendary gaffer Alex Ferguson led Manchester United to eight FA Cup finals, which is a record – and won five of them.

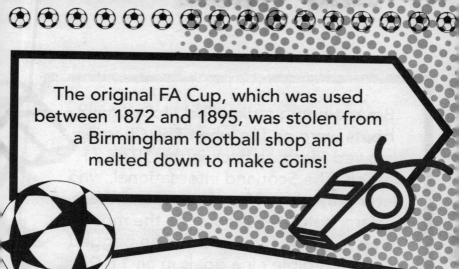

The original FA Cup, which was used between 1872 and 1895, was stolen from a Birmingham football shop and melted down to make coins!

18

The youngest goalscorer in an FA Cup final was Man. United's Norman Whiteside. The Northern Ireland star was just 18 years and 19 days old when he netted for The Red Devils against Brighton!

Cardiff became the only non-English team to have won the FA Cup when they beat Arsenal 1–0 at Wembley in 1927!

Bournemouth striker Ted McDougall's boots were on fire when The Cherries played Margate back in the 1970–71 season. The Scotland international, who later played for Man. United and West Ham, holds the record for the most goals in an FA Cup tie when he bagged an incredible nine goals in an 11–0 win in the first round.

25

The record for the fastest goal in an FA Cup final belongs to Louis Saha, who scored after just 25 seconds for Everton against Chelsea in the 2009 Cup final. It didn't do any good, though – Chelsea went on to win 2–1!

Tottenham's Gary Mabbutt, Man. City's Tommy Hutchinson and Charlton's Bert Turner have all scored for their team AND the opposition in an FA Cup final!

In the 1956 FA Cup final, Man. City keeper Bert Trautmann played on after breaking a bone in his neck in the 75th minute!

TICKET

The first keeper to save a penalty in an FA Cup final was Wimbledon stopper Dave Beasant! The Dons skipper dived to his left to save a John Aldridge spot kick with Wimbledon winning 1–0, and they held on to their lead to produce one of the biggest shocks in FA Cup history!

The first penalty shoot-out in an FA Cup final came in 2005, when Arsenal beat Man. United 5–4 after a 0–0 snooze-fest at the Millennium Stadium.

The 1923 final between Bolton and West Ham was the first to be played at Wembley, and there were so many people at the game that fans had to be cleared from the pitch by mounted police. The match has been known as the 'White Horse Final' ever since because of the famous police horse, Billie, that cleared fans from the pitch.

4

At the first tournament in 1960, there were only four teams in the finals – now there are 24!

The 1992 European Championship in Sweden was the first major tournament where the players had their names as well as numbers on the back of their shirts!

15

Euro 2016 will be the 15th Euros, and the third to be held in France!

The first tournament was almost cancelled because of a lack of support from countries – many were too late applying to take part!

The biggest attendance in the history of the competition came when Scotland played England in 1968 – a massive 134,461 squeezed into Hampden Park to see a 1–1 draw!

0

England have never won their first game at a Euro finals, drawing four and losing four! Can they break the record against Russia?

In 1968, the semi-final between Italy and the USSR was decided by the toss of a coin! Italy guessed right and made it through to the final!

44

Yugoslavia substitute Mateja Kezman was sent off after only 44 seconds against Norway at Euro 2000!

The oldest player to appear in the competition is Germany's Lothar Matthaus, who was 39 years and 91 days when he made his last appearance!

3

Spain and Germany have both won the competition three times, which is a joint record!

Dutch keeper Edwin van der Sar went an incredible 12 years without conceding a goal in the competition, racking up nine clean sheets between 1996 and 2008!

19

The youngest player to appear in a final is Cristiano Ronaldo, who was just 19 years and 150 days old when he played for Portugal against Greece in 2004. They lost 1–0, though!

1

In 2012, Spain became the first team in the history of the competition to win it twice in a row!

68

Russia's Dmitri Kirichenko scored after just 68 seconds in their game against Greece in 2004 – it's the fastest goal in the history of the competition!

Vladimir Smicer, whose goal put the Czech Republic into the quarter-finals of Euro 96, flew back to Prague straight after the game – to get married! He returned two days later to play in his country's win over Portugal!

3

Only three nations have won the tournament they have hosted – Spain in 1964, Italy in 1968 and France in 1984!

43

Germany have played 43 matches in the European Championship finals – that's more than any other country!

In 2004, Portugal became the first host nation to lose in the final when they were beaten 1–0 by Greece!

In the same final, Greece became the first country to win the competition with a foreign coach – Otto Rehhagel was German!

18

France legend Michel Platini holds the record for the fastest hat-trick in the competition after netting a treble in just 18 minutes against Yugloslavia at the 1984 finals!

In 1964, Holland were dumped out of the tournament by Luxembourg! The tiny country, which has a population of just over 500,000, didn't win another European Championship qualifier until 1995!

Portugal are probably the unluckiest European Championship team ever. They've made it at least as far as the semi-finals four times, but have never won it!

16

Yugoslavia legend Dragan Stojkovic first played in the European Championships in France in 1984, but then had to wait another 16 years – Euro 2000 – for his next game in the finals!

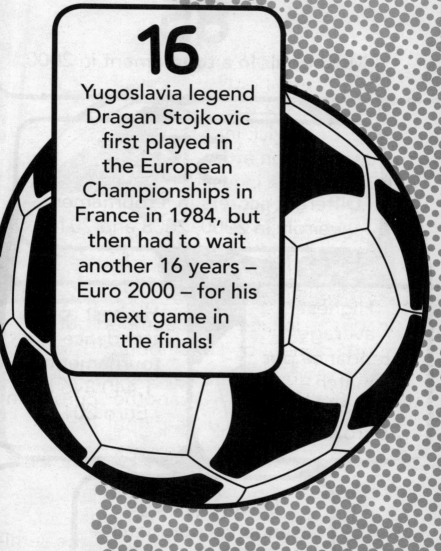

85

Most goals in a tournament in 2000.

53

Different scorers in a tournament –
weirdly in 2000, 2008 and 2012.

Highest average attendance per match – 59,847 in Euro 1968.

Highest total attendance in a tournament – 1,440,846 in Euro 2012.

Lowest average attendance per match – 19,740 in Euro 1960.

WINS

3	Spain
3	Germany
2	France
1	Soviet Union
1	Holland
1	Italy
1	Greece
1	Denmark
1	Czechoslovakia

TOP GOALSCORERS

1	**Michel Platini**	France	9 goals
2	**Alan Shearer**	England	7 goals
3=	**Ruud Van Nistelrooy**	Holland	6 goals
3=	**Patrick Kluivert**	Holland	6 goals
3=	**Zlatan Ibrahimovic**	Sweden	6 goals
3=	**Thierry Henry**	France	6 goals
3=	**Cristiano Ronaldo**	Portugal	6 goals
3=	**Nuno Gomes**	Portugal	6 goals
9=	**Savo Milosevic**	Serbia	5 goals
9=	**Wayne Rooney**	England	5 goals